For Joseph and Jacob
P.L.
For Nesta
E.C.C.

First American edition

Library of Congress Catalog Card Number 88-81824
10 9 8 7 6 5 4 3 2 1

First published in Great Britain in 1989
by Walker Books Ltd., London

Printed in Italy

Cissy Lavender

Primrose Lockwood   Emma Chichester Clark

Little, Brown and Company
Boston · Toronto · London

Cissy Lavender was just wondering where to go for her vacation when she saw a rather interesting advertisement in the Saturday morning newspaper. It read:

Gentleman requires housekeeper
to care for his house, cats
and dog, for ten days
at the beginning of August.
Country situation.

"I've never had a housekeeping vacation," said Cissy Lavender. And she was so excited about the idea (and the cats and the dog and the country situation) that she wrote back at once.

It wasn't long before a reply came. It said:

Dear Cissy Lavender,
                    I am sure I cannot leave my house in
more expert hands.
                              Yours thankfully,
                              William Holly

Then at the very bottom it said:

    P.S. Take care the dog doesn't gobble the cats' food.
Enclosed was a large brass key.

Cissy Lavender wasn't sure what a housekeeper should take on vacation, but to be extra certain, as well as clothes she packed:

one feather duster
one sewing basket
one paint brush
one can of shiny green paint
one bolt of material
one roll of ribbon
one oval pan
one clothes' line
and a large bag of lavender.

"I wonder if there'll be anything else I'll need," said Cissy Lavender.

On the journey Cissy Lavender wondered what the cats and dog were called and whether they'd like being looked after by a housekeeper instead of a gentleman.

The cats were called Peter and Posy and they purred.

The dog was called Mistletoe and he barked. But after five whole minutes he lifted up his paw and made friends.

The gentleman had left a note on the kitchen table for Cissy Lavender, saying:

If you have anything of importance to tell me, I am staying at the above address...

"I expect I shall have lots of importance to tell the gentleman," said Cissy Lavender.

In fact she wrote him a letter the very next day.

It came about because Peter went up the chimney in the library when Cissy Lavender was reading and dusting books.

"I think that must be a thing of great importance to tell the gentleman," said Cissy Lavender.

So she wrote:

Dear William Holly,

Peter climbed up the chimney today when I was dusting in the library. He came back down but I'm sorry to say he's just a bit blacker than usual.

Best wishes,

Cissy Lavender

P.S. I think you have some very interesting books.

The next day Cissy Lavender thought she'd darn some socks for the gentleman. The socks were green but she could only find red wool in her sewing basket.

"I'd better tell the gentleman," thought Cissy Lavender. So she wrote:

Dear William Holly,

Today I mended all your socks, only I didn't have any green wool so I mended them in red instead. You'll be pleased to know the red parts look just like holly berries.

Very best wishes,

Cissy Lavender

P.S. The dog has only gobbled the cats' food once so far.

When the next day came Cissy Lavender thought she'd give the back door a new coat of shiny green paint.

"I'd better write and tell the gentleman," said Cissy Lavender. So she wrote:

Dear William Holly,
When I was painting the back door today, Posy stuck her paw in the green paint, then ran off down the path. The paw prints look like little green holly leaves on the paving stones.

Very very best wishes,

Cissy Lavender

P.S. The dog has gobbled the cats' food twice now.

The following day Cissy Lavender found some ripe red raspberries at the bottom of the garden.

"I'll make them into jam for the gentleman," said Cissy Lavender.

Afterwards, she wrote:

Dear William Holly,
                    Today I made you five jars of raspberry jam. If you don't like raspberry jam it doesn't matter because your cats and dog like it an enormous amount.

Very very very best wishes,

Cissy Lavender

P.S. I hope the cats are allowed on the kitchen table.

The next day Cissy Lavender thought she'd make some curtains for the garden shed.

"I'll write and tell the gentleman," said Cissy Lavender. She wrote:

Dear William Holly,

Today I made some curtains for the garden shed. They're green, so I know you'll be as pleased as anything when you see them. And I've tied them back with lavender ribbons.

Very very very very best wishes,

Cissy Lavender

P.S. The dog has gobbled the cats' food three times now.

The next day Cissy Lavender washed all the gentleman's sheets, towels and tablecloths.

"I'd better write and tell the gentleman," said Cissy Lavender. She wrote:

Dear William Holly,

    Today I washed all your sheets, towels and tablecloths. I'm sorry to say all the color ran out of your towels and now all your sheets are green. I hope you won't mind too much. They're a very pretty shade of green.
    Very very very very very best wishes,

Cissy Lavender

P.S. Have you ever tried hanging out washing with a cat sitting on your head?

The next day Cissy Lavender thought she'd dig a pond in the garden for the gentleman.

"I'd better write and tell him," said Cissy Lavender. So she wrote:

Dear William Holly,

You'll be pleased to know you've now got a big pond at the bottom of your garden. It's a very nice pond with flowers growing around it. If you don't like ponds you'll have to remember that frogs and toads like them, and so do housekeepers – for dangling their feet in.

Very very very very very very best wishes,

Cissy Lavender

P.S. I forgot to bring my own spade so I borrowed yours. I expect you're such an understanding gentleman that you won't mind one bit.

The next day Cissy Lavender wrote yet another letter to the gentleman. It said:

Dear William Holly,
        It occurred to me today that gentlemen might not like sitting with their feet dangling in ponds like housekeepers, so I've made you a garden seat instead. I'm afraid it did take all the wood left in the woodshed, but it's such an attractive garden seat, I don't think you'll mind that when you see it.
        Very very very very very very very best wishes,

Cissy Lavender

P.S. I'm thinking of writing a book called *All You Need to Know about Housekeeping*. You see, I've found that spades and hammers are just as important as clothes' lines and preserving pans. Would you like a copy, William Holly?

The next day Cissy Lavender was so busy making little green lavender bags to put under the pillows in the gentleman's room that she forgot all about the cats and afterwards found them lying comfortably on the gentleman's bed.

"It's a good thing it's too late to write and tell the gentleman," said Cissy Lavender.

On the last day, instead of sending a letter to the gentleman, Cissy Lavender got one from him instead. It said:

Dear Cissy Lavender,
                I shall be back in time for tea.
Thank you for caring for my house and cats and dog.
I can't wait to see:

my dusted library
my hollyberry socks
my shiny green door
my holly leaf path
my five jars of jam
my garden shed curtains
my green washed sheets
my frog and toad pond
and my wooden garden seat.

Yours curiously,

William Holly

P.S. Thank you for all your letters too!

Cissy Lavender was so pleased with the letter and thought the gentleman such a kind gentleman that she began at once to prepare him an extra special tea.

She made:

pea soup
cucumber sandwiches
lettuce and radish salad
and redcurrant jelly.

She baked:

apple dumplings
raspberry tart
gooseberry pie
and cherry buns.

She put on the table:

the best green cloth
the best green plates
a bowl of red roses
and a cake decorated with holly leaves.

And instead of a lavender dress, she wore a green one.
"Now everything is ready," said Cissy Lavender.

The gentleman arrived just in time for tea. He wore:

a green suit
a green shirt
a green tie
a green spotted handkerchief
a green hat band on his hat
green shoes and stockings...
but in his buttonhole he wore a sprig of lavender.

The gentleman was a very nice gentleman and he liked the tea and Cissy Lavender so much, he asked if she would come and visit again some time.

Cissy Lavender replied, "Certainly."

P.S. You'll be pleased to know that Cissy Lavender hasn't only been once, but lots of times. Sometimes she sits with her feet in the pond and, in case you're wondering, the gentleman doesn't mind sitting with his feet in the pond either.

As for the gentleman's cats and the gentleman's dog – they're rather more dignified.